Dedicated to our own wonderful grandmothers

978-1-933212-35-7

Published by Commonwealth Editions, an imprint of Applewood Books, Inc.,
Box 27, Carlisle, Massachusetts 01741

Visit us on the web at www.commonwealtheditions.com
Visit Shankman and O'Neill on the web at www.shankmanoneill.com

"Kristenalwaysnotsonormal" font created by Nic Koeck via FontPanda.com
"Rumpelstiltskin" font created by David Kerkhoff
Watercolor photoshop brushes by McBadshoes: mcbadshoes.deviantart.com

Printed in China.

10 9 8 7 6 5 4 3 2 1

My Grandma Lives in Florida

by
Ed Shankman

illustrated by
Dave O'Neill

Commonwealth Editions
Carlisle, Massachusetts

My grandma lives in Florida,
And that is where we go
When Daddy says he cannot stand
Another inch of snow.

'Cause Florida's the Sunshine State,
And that's what makes that state so great.
The sun down there is big and bold
And round and warm and bright as gold.

And right beneath that golden sun is Grandma's house—the yellow one.
(Houses are lovely all over the nation, but under the sun is my favorite location!)

When we go inside, Grandma gives me a kiss.
In fact, there's no place on my face she will miss.
I may wriggle and giggle and grumble and hiss.
But only a grandma can kiss you like this.

Then after she hugs me with all of her might,
She looks me all over and laughs with delight.
She squeezes my cheeks and she ruffles my hair,
And she tells me how happy she is that I'm there.

(It's a lot to put up with, but as you can see,
I love my grandma and Grandma loves me.)

She says that I grew and I'm so handsome, too,
And I look very much like my dad used to do.
And maybe that's true but it strikes me as weird,
Because I'm very small and I don't have a beard.

She brings me a pear and the old teddy bear
And the big box of crayons she keeps for me there.
And then, while I color, she reads me some rhymes
That she's read to me, happily, hundreds of times.

There are rhymes about giants and witches and kings—
About pirates with parrots and angels with wings.
And those rhymes, when they're read, ring like chimes in my head,
Which makes rhyming the best way a thing can be said.

After all, as you know, a word's only a word.
And a word, by itself, disappears once it's heard.
But you put that same word at the end of a rhyme,
And, my friends, it remains in our brains for all time!

Grandma gives me the room with the big fluffy bed
And a big fluffy pillow just right for my head.
And that's all I recall because in the next minute,
My dream has arrived and I'm already in it.

This morning we grab all the foods we can reach,
And we pack ourselves off to a Florida beach!
The sand all around us is gleaming and white
'Cause the sun overhead is so brilliantly bright.

It shines like a beam on the Florida crowd
Down from Altamonte Springs to Kissimmee/St. Cloud.
Til every last shiver of coldness is gone
From Lake Okeechobee to Boca Raton.

From Neptune Beach to Cocoa Beach
And West Palm Beach to Vero Beach,
That sun warms each beach it can reach.
And rest assured it reaches each!

It shines on every manatee
From Tampa Bay to Longboat Key,
And every bass and ballyhoo,
And on the barracudas, too.

It shines on the gators that play in the bay
And the waiters that wait in the outdoor cafe.
To tell you the truth, if the weather was gray,
I'm not sure that the gators or waiters would stay.

But the weather's not gray. No, it's not gray at all.
This isn't New Jersey, New York, or St. Paul.
This is Florida, baby, and there's only one.
And when you're in Florida, you're in the sun!

My grandma is wearing her big floppy hat,
And her sunglasses aren't much smaller than that.
Her robe is so fluffy she looks like a cat,
And she wonders out loud if it makes her look fat.

"No fatter than yesterday, Grandma," I say.
"You look just the same as you do every day."
And that makes her laugh, which I find quite confusing.
I can't always tell why she thinks I'm amusing.

But this is the thing that makes grandmothers grand:
They love you for reasons you can't understand.
My grandmother thinks that I'm clever and cute.
If I stand on my head. If I blow on a flute.

If I say funny things

or I make funny faces.

Or if I sneak into ridiculous places.

Or play with my nose

or my toes or my toys,

Or today when I made an unusual noise.

Whatever I do, Grandma claps and she shrieks,
And she tells all her neighbors about it for weeks!

There are others who think I'm alright or okay,
And a few who'd prefer that I just go away.
But I'm the best thing in my grandmother's day.
And they say that's the way things are likely to stay.

I jump in the waves and I'm having a ball.
My grandma "wades" in, which means hardly at all.
She takes tiny steps holding onto my shoulder.
(I guess when you're older the water is colder.)

After a while we go for a walk,
Just my grandma and me, because we like to talk.
She tells me the names of the flowers and birds.
She sings a few songs, and she knows all the words.

She talks about life in the old days and how
The world was much different than how it is now.
But even back then they had beaches and sun,
And it sounds like they found a few ways to have fun.

It all seems quite strange, as we walk by the sea,
That my grandma was once just as little as me.
But growing, I guess, is just something we do.
And I think, before long, it could happen to you!

She tells me a joke and she gives me a hug.
She points out a clam and a crab and a bug.
I find her a shell and she smiles so wide
That I think she has Florida sunshine inside!

The next week or so, we are busy as bees
Seeing all of the sights that a sightseer sees.
If you like seeing sights, I am begging you please,
You must make your way down here and see some of these!

With so many ways to have fun in the sun,
You can run to each one and still never be done.
The doing, the seeing—it's all very freeing,
And sometimes the best fun of all is just being.

So at times we just be—Grandma, Daddy, and me.
We just be in the house or we be by the sea.
And I see, as we be, that we're happy together.
And happy is easy in Florida weather.

Now some states are known for a bird or a plant,
They can choose what they like, I'm not saying they can't.
But down here in Florida, gators are king.
And if you're fond of beasts, then a gator's the thing!

A gator is great from the jaws to the gizzard.
Why, only a wizard could make such a lizard!
With sharp pointy teeth and our tails and our scales,
We're much cooler than woodchucks or llamas or snails.

Some folks may like turtles. Or maybe a pheasant.
And I'm sure a pheasant is perfectly pleasant.
To be very clear, I am no pheasant hater.
A pheasant is fine, but a gator is greater.

Yes, a beast of our kind is uniquely designed.
Take a look at the way all our teeth are aligned.
And the claws on our paws are so perfectly shined,
That they may be the shiniest kind you will find!

Now, let's say you're seeking a cool souvenir
To remind you of all the good times you had here.

Well, whether you purchase a bag or a bonnet,
You'll probably find that a gator is on it.

Someday I'll move here for good—wait and see!
'Cause it's the best place for a gator to be.
But the moment has come that the visit is done,
And we must say farewell to the Florida sun.

If you travel like I do, I think you will learn
That while travel is nice, it is nice to return.
So after I'm coddled and cuddled and kissed,
We head back to our home and the things that we've missed.

And though I'm no longer in Florida now,
The great Sunshine State is still with me somehow,
'Cause I have a picture of my grandma's face
And Florida gators all over the place.

The End

ALSO by Ed Shankman and Dave O'Neill

The Boston Balloonies
The Cods of Cape Cod
I Met a Moose in Maine One Day
Champ and Me by the Maple Tree
The Bourbon Street Band is Back

ALSO by Ed Shankman with Dave Frank

I Went to the Party in Kalamazoo

Ed Shankman

Ed's entire life has been one continuous creative project. In addition to writing, playing music, and painting, he is the chief creative officer for an advertising agency, where he helps others discover and focus their own creative voices. Ed was very close to his own grandmothers, Mal and Sarah. So it is with great affection that he presents this homage to the very special relationship between children and their grandmothers.

Dave O'Neill

Dave O'Neill is an illustrator and Art Director working in New York City. He began drawing when he was a child and is thankful that he never stopped. His brain is firmly anchored in cartoons and pop culture, and he moonlights as an improv comedian. Throughout the years, Dave has worked with several agencies, the first of which is where he met Ed Shankman. Though he has applied his creative strengths to advertising and marketing alike, he admits that drawing children's books is certainly the most fun. Dave resides in NJ with Melinda, the super-cool girl he married. They are the proud owners of a keyboard she won on Double Dare.

www.shankmanoneill.com